Hello Kitty

and friends

The Halloween Parade

·A HELLO KITTY ADVENTURE·

Hello Kitty
and friends

The Halloween Parade

·A HELLO KITTY ADVENTURE·

HarperCollins *Children's Books*

MEET

Hello Kitty

and friends

Mimmy

Hello Kitty

Tammy

Mama

Papa

Grandpa

Grandma

Fifi

Dear Daniel

Boo

With special thanks to
Linda Chapman and Michelle Misra

First published in Great Britain by HarperCollins *Children's Books* in 2014

www.harpercollins.co.uk
1 3 5 7 9 10 8 6 4 2
ISBN: 978-0-00-754245-1

Printed and bound in England by Clays Ltd, St Ives plc.

Conditions of Sale

MIX
Paper from
responsible sources
FSC™ C007454

FSC™ is a non-profit international organisation established to promote
the responsible management of the world's forests. Products carrying the
FSC label are independently certified to assure consumers that they come
from forests that are managed to meet the social, economic and
ecological needs of present and future generations,
and other controlled sources.

Find out more about HarperCollins and the environment at
www.harpercollins.co.uk/green

Contents

Picnic Fun!

Hello Kitty smiled as she spread out a checked rug on the grass. Today was going to be *perfect*. She hadn't seen her friends Tammy and Fifi for a while, because it had been the school holidays and they had all been busy.

That afternoon they were coming over for a picnic and she couldn't wait to catch up! Quickly, she placed the little paper plates and cups on the rug, then she wound some pink fairy lights around the trunk of the apple tree.

Mama smiled at her as Hello Kitty ran back inside to get the food. She'd been *wondering* where she'd got to.

Hello Kitty picked up the jug of fruit punch and a plate of sandwiches from the table and put them carefully on a tray as she explained that she'd just been making sure everything was just right for her friends. Fifi and Tammy would be there any minute.

Mama balanced some rainbow-iced cupcakes on top of the tray too. Hello Kitty wouldn't want to forget those!

Hello Kitty grinned and thanked her, trying to keep everything steady as she made her way back outside.

Tammy and Fifi were two of Hello Kitty's **best** friends in the world, along with her twin sister, Mimmy, and her oldest friend, Dear Daniel. Dear Daniel was away at the moment travelling with his dad, a photographer. He'd been gone for the last two weeks. Hello Kitty smiled as she thought about Tammy, Fifi and Dear Daniel. They were all in the same class at school and had started the Friendship Club. They met at each other's houses to do fun things, like drawing, painting and baking.

Hello Kitty heard the doorbell ring and ran back inside. She threw the door open.

What a **surprise!** Tammy had a plate of biscuits and Fifi was carrying a big plate of red jelly covered with sprinkles.

Hello Kitty had told her friends not to bring

anything! But she didn't mind that they had. She

happily gave them both a hug.

Tammy and Fifi smiled. They knew Hello Kitty

would have had everything for them, but they

wanted to bring something *anyway*.

Hello Kitty led them through the house to

the garden, so they could see what she had

ready for them. She showed them out through

the back door, then stepped aside so they could

see what she had set up. **Ta da!**

Fifi and Tammy gasped.

It was beautiful! They both laughed, and gave

Hello Kitty another hug. They had missed her

so much.

Hello Kitty and friends

Hello Kitty laughed too, and poured them each a drink as she asked them about their holidays. What had they both been doing?

Fifi chattered away excitedly. She had been doing a lot of ice-skating! Hello Kitty wasn't surprised. She knew how much Fifi **loved** to skate. She turned to Tammy – what had she been up to?

Tammy had been hanging out with Timmy, her twin brother. They had been to the park and the cinema, and had lots of fun together.

And what had Hello Kitty been doing, they

wanted to know?

Hello Kitty had some really

exciting news to share! It

was Halloween soon –

and she'd just been asked

to be on a committee to

organise a Fancy-Dress

Parade. Fifi squealed.

A Halloween Parade? How **exciting!**

Hello Kitty nodded. It was exciting! It was to

raise money for charity, and there were going

to be music and games. There were even going

to be prizes for the best costumes!

Hello Kitty *and friends*

Tammy and Fifi wanted to know if they could come along.

Hello Kitty smiled. Of course they could! She had the first meeting tomorrow. Oh, and there was something else $SUPER$ exciting… a letter had come that morning! She pulled an envelope from her pocket and held it out. It had a foreign-looking stamp and familiar handwriting.

It was a letter from Dear Daniel!

Hello Kitty had saved it to open with her friends. She handed it to Fifi, so that she could read it out.

Fifi's eyes sparkled as she opened the envelope slowly.

Tammy and Hello Kitty giggled. Come on, Fifi!

Fifi started to read.

'Dear Hello Kitty, Tammy and Fifi,' the letter said.

'By the time you get this, I'll be deep in the Amazon jungle…' How amazing!

'We're going to be taking a boat tomorrow so I'm on the lookout for crocodiles and monkeys. Today we saw snakes and lizards...'

Tammy squealed.

Snakes!

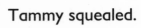

Fifi continued

to read.

'It's so great here. I keep thinking about all the things you might be doing back at home without me though. Write back soon. Love, Dear Daniel.'

How nice! They were all touched at how much it sounded like Dear Daniel was missing

them. They were really missing him too!

Oooh! Hello Kitty had an idea; they should write him a letter straight back, and send him a present. Fifi had a great suggestion too – the present could be something to do with nature! Dear Daniel loved bugs and creepy crawlies.

Hello Kitty giggled. She wasn't sure the postman would like it if they posted a box of spiders! Tammy thought hard. It needed to be something small and light…

Ah ha! Hello Kitty gasped. What about a friendship bracelet?

Brilliant! What would they need? Fifi had lots of questions; she had never made a bracelet before.

Hello Kitty made a list in her head. They would need beads, cord, glue, a clasp… She knew about making jewellery because she and her Mama made it *together* at home. She could ask Mama if they could have some materials.

GLUE

And they could meet again tomorrow to make it! Tammy clapped her hands excitedly.

But Hello Kitty had the Halloween Parade meeting then. **Soon** though – how about the day after that?

That would be perfect! They all smiled at each other. Hello Kitty picked up her cup of

Hello Kitty and friends

fruit punch, and raised it up so she and her friends could toast each other.

To the friendship club – the most SUPER club in the world!

Getting Organised

So... what colour should Dear Daniel's bracelet be? The girls were still trying to decide as Fifi spread out cotton cords on Hello Kitty's bedroom floor, when the Friendship Club met two days later.

Tammy suggested red – that was Dear Daniel's favourite; so Hello Kitty picked the red cord up and started knotting it together to make the bracelet.

As she worked, they **chattered** away – Tammy wanted to know how Hello Kitty's parade meeting had gone... was everything getting organised?

Hello Kitty smiled. It had been brilliant! There were a couple of adults on the committee who were running it; they were organising the tables and other **big** things. But Hello Kitty and two other girls were doing everything else.

Who were the other girls? Fifi wanted
to know.

Hello Kitty told Tammy and Fifi all about
them; their names were
Claudia and Susie, and they
were **great!** Claudia
was really good fun. She
could do five cartwheels
in a row! And Susie – well,
she was great too. She loved
cheerleading and she could flip over
backwards. They should see her! Hello Kitty
thought Fifi and Tammy would really like
them both.

Tammy was still curious though – what about the parade? Did she know what she was going to dress as?

Hello Kitty shook her head. She was still wondering what she should go as... She and Mimmy had both dressed as pumpkins last year. She pointed at a photo on the wall, and Tammy and Fifi giggled – Hello Kitty looked so cute! She

wasn't sure what she'd wear this year though, but as it was Halloween, everyone could wear whatever costume they wanted! She was really excited about it.

Fifi **grinned**. She knew what she would go as then, she already had the perfect costume at home... an ice-skater, of course!

They all giggled.

Tammy wasn't sure what she would go as either; maybe something

scary? But she wanted some more details. What
was Hello Kitty doing for the parade – what did
she need to organise?

Hello Kitty
thought hard. She
was doing some
of the decorations,
organising the judges
and prizes and putting up posters.
Claudia was in charge of the music
and designing the posters. Susie was
doing the balloons, some of the decorations
too, and was sorting out the prize table.
Phew – there was lots to do!

Hello Kitty *and friends*

Hello Kitty was also going to ask her Grandpa and Miss Davey, their class teacher, to judge the costumes – they would be *perfect* for it. And she thought she'd get some little silver cups as prizes…

She was chatting away and working on the bracelet when Mama called up the stairs to her. She had a phone call!

Hello Kitty wondered who it was. And she was right in the middle of a knot too… Could Tammy take over? Hello Kitty smiled.

Tammy nodded as Hello Kitty rushed down the stairs and answered the phone. It was her new friend Susie!

How could she help?

Hello Kitty listened to Susie's question. **Oh, yes**... she knew where Susie could buy balloons – the Non-Stop Party Shop! She'd been there lots of times.

Susie started talking again – asking about colours and themes and whether the balloons should be silver and gold.

Hmmm... Susie chatted on. Finally, Hello Kitty looked at her watch. She'd been on the phone for **fifteen minutes!**

She'd better go! She'd see Susie tomorrow. They could look at balloons together then.

She rushed up the stairs, and apologised for taking so long. So, should they get back to work and finish the friendship bracelet?

Fifi held it out. They had just finished it!

Hello Kitty smiled and thanked them both. Since the bracelet was finished, should they write the letter to go with it instead?

But just then, Mimmy poked her head round the door. Tammy's mum had arrived to pick her

up! Tammy jumped up. They would have to do the letter another time.

But they still needed to plan their next meeting. Hmmm. Hello Kitty couldn't meet tomorrow; she'd just said she'd go with Susie to look at balloons. And she couldn't do Wednesday either as she was making decorations!

What about Thursday, Hello Kitty suggested – would that work?

Fifi looked puzzled. They had been going to go bowling then, for Tammy's birthday. Didn't Hello Kitty remember?

Oh – of course she did! Hello Kitty remembered now; they'd arranged it ages ago.

But… could they do the letter at the same time?

Fifi smiled. That would be perfect.

Tammy rushed for the door. She had to go – her mum was waiting. But she'd **_definitely_** love to work on the letter on Thursday!

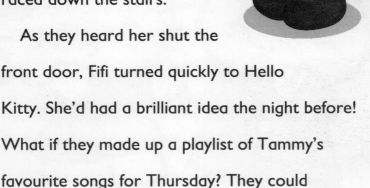

She called goodbye as she raced down the stairs.

As they heard her shut the front door, Fifi turned quickly to Hello Kitty. She'd had a brilliant idea the night before! What if they made up a playlist of Tammy's favourite songs for Thursday? They could buy the songs and give it to Tammy for her birthday! Fifi's dad had said he'd show her how to do it if they worked out what songs they'd like. Tammy would **love** it!

Hello Kitty nodded, grinning; she definitely would, and it sounded like a nice idea.

It would be better if they could get together to do it, said Fifi, but Hello Kitty was so busy over the next few days...

Hello Kitty nodded. She looked so worried that Fifi quickly reassured her that she could put it together on her own.

Phew! Hello Kitty thanked her, feeling relieved. That would be wonderful. There was just so much to do with the Halloween parade...

But Fifi smiled. She would sort it out for them. Hello Kitty didn't need to worry! But she'd better go. Fifi gave a quick wave as she got up and left.

Hello Kitty waved back as Fifi went downstairs.

At the last minute she remembered she wanted to ask Fifi about a card for Tammy...

She *raced* out of her room, but Fifi had already gone. Hello Kitty turned and went slowly back into her bedroom. She was sure it would be fine!

So Much to Do!

The days flew by. There was just so much to organise for the Halloween parade. Hello Kitty didn't mind too much though, as Claudia and Susie were so much **fun!** She spent lots of time with them, working on everything they needed to do.

On Thursday afternoon, she was just about to leave her house to meet Fifi and Tammy for bowling when Claudia rang.

Claudia was in a panic. There had been a total and complete **disaster!** The band that was going to play at the parade couldn't make it. Could Hello Kitty come round for a meeting straightaway?

Hmmm. Hello Kitty bit her lip. She was supposed to be going bowling, she explained...

But Claudia sounded really worried; this was super-important! Could Hello Kitty *pleeeeasssse* come and help her and Susie work it out? They didn't know what to do without her!

Well then; Hello Kitty didn't want to let Fifi and Tammy down but this was an emergency, so she knew they'd understand. She'd come round now. Claudia said thanks, and Hello Kitty put the phone down just as Mama came in. Was she ready to go bowling?

Hello Kitty explained about the call and the emergency.

Could Mama please take her to Claudia's house instead?

Mama was *surprised*.

But what about bowling with Tammy and Fifi?

Hello Kitty promised Mama she would ring them when she got to Claudia's and tell them she couldn't make it. She was sure they'd understand. They were such good friends, of

course they would! Although Hello Kitty did feel like she was forgetting something.

Mama wasn't sure, but if Hello Kitty thought it would be OK... especially since it was such an emergency. She opened the door and waited for Hello Kitty to follow her out to the car.

Hang on... she just needed to find her parade notebook! Hello Kitty ran upstairs to grab it, and raced back down to go...

All the way to Claudia's house, Hello Kitty thought about the band. What were they going to do? She made some notes and hoped Susie

and Claudia were thinking as hard as she was!

When she arrived at Claudia's house,

Claudia flung the door open. **Hooray**,

she was here! Claudia hugged Hello Kitty and

started chattering away excitedly. Susie was

upstairs, and they'd been painting their nails.

What colour did Hello Kitty like best? She showed Hello Kitty her hands. Half her nails were painted in silver and half in pink. Weren't they cool?

Hello Kitty said yes, but she was surprised. She had thought that Susie and Claudia would have been looking at possible bands!

Claudia took Hello Kitty's hand, and pulled her upstairs. She had to have her nails done now. Normally Hello Kitty loved painting her nails but today her head was full of their parade problem. What about the band? Shouldn't they be trying to sort that out?

But Claudia said firmly that they could do it once they'd done their nails!

Hmmm, OK. Hello Kitty still wasn't sure what to think as Claudia bounded on up the stairs. She followed her slowly.

Susie called out to them as they walked in. She waved a nail polish pot at Hello Kitty. What colour did she want her nails to be?

Hello Kitty joined in with painting her nails, but tried to be quick. She started to ask what they should do about the band, but Susie squealed and spoke quickly. Her favourite band at the moment was The Fizzy Pops! Wouldn't it be *amazing* if they played at the parade?

Hello Kitty agreed that it would be completely SUPER, but they were probably too famous to play at this parade though. They needed to come up with a band they could get.

They all thought hard for a minute, and then
Claudia gasped! Her cousin was in a band.
Perhaps she could come and play, or at least
she would know someone who would. She could
sort it all out!

Hello Kitty sighed in relief. That would
be great! There was just so much to do and
remember at the moment, especially with the

parade and deciding on a costume, which she still had **no idea** about...

Claudia smiled. They could leave the band to her. Now – they should all do their hair next. It was time they had some fun!

A Scary Mistake

Hello Kitty, Claudia and Susie styled each other's hair and then went outside into Claudia's **lovely** garden. They sat down and talked about their outfits for the parade. Claudia and Susie were going to go as matching

cheerleaders with red
skirts and white tops,
and tie their hair up
in ponytails with red
and white ribbons.

But Hello Kitty still wasn't
sure what she would go as. She wished
that they had done a bit more for the parade
that afternoon, but at least they had had fun,
and Claudia didn't seem worried any more. She
opened her notebook and made a new list of
things to do.

She checked down the list. So, Claudia would
get the band sorted now?

Claudia assured her she would.

And Susie would get the rest of the decorations sorted. Oh – and would she also organise the balloons being blown up on Saturday morning?

Susie smiled. **Definitely!**

Hello Kitty beamed back at her.

It was all coming together. She had

done the prizes already, and she had the judges.

She would also put more posters up. And they

could meet early Saturday morning to set up!

She said goodbye and *ran* out to meet

Mama who had just arrived in the car. She

called out hi, and told her all about how they'd

had the best afternoon – and had figured out
what to do about the band!

Mama nodded and smiled, but was quiet.

Whatever could be the matter? And then
as Mama started to speak, she suddenly
remembered! She had forgotten to phone
Tammy and Fifi and tell them she wasn't going
bowling! They had called Mama to find out what
was going on – they had been a bit worried
about her.

Oh no! Hello
Kitty gasped. She
had completely
forgotten! She had

been so busy thinking about the band and what they needed to do for the parade.

Mama told her not to worry – they hadn't minded once she had explained what had happened. But Hello Kitty should call them when they got back.

Hello Kitty nodded; she'd call them as soon as she got in. Mama **smiled.**

As soon as they got home, Hello Kitty

went to the phone and called Fifi. When she
answered, Hello Kitty said hello, and quickly
explained how **sorry** she was about missing
bowling, and how she had meant to call and
tell them she couldn't make it, but she'd just
completely forgotten... she was so sorry they
had needed to call Mama! Fifi told her not to
worry. But had she forgotten what day it
was too?

Hmmm...

Fifi blurted it out. It was Tammy's birthday!

Hello Kitty clapped her hand over her mouth.

Oh no! How could she have forgotten? She'd

just been so busy!

Hello Kitty was so sorry; she apologised

to Fifi again. She had just been so busy that

she had forgotten. But she would call

Tammy straightaway and

apologise to her too.

She could hear Fifi

smile as she spoke.

She was sure it

would be fine!

Hello Kitty *and friends*

It was still Tammy's birthday — Hello Kitty should definitely give her a call.

Hello Kitty said she would. She felt **really** bad about forgetting.

Fifi kept talking. She and Tammy had written Dear Daniel's letter too, and sent it off with the

bracelet, so Hello Kitty didn't need to worry about that either.

They really were the best! Hello Kitty was so grateful that she had such amazing friends. She thanked Fifi and said goodbye as she put down the phone.

Hello Kitty couldn't *believe* that she'd forgotten Tammy's birthday! Normally she was so organised, but with so much on it was hard to remember everything. How could she ever make this right?

Hello Kitty rang Tammy straightaway. She

61

explained how sorry she was that she hadn't been at bowling, and that she had forgotten it was her birthday. But thank goodness she'd still had time to call – *Happy Birthday!*

Tammy thanked and reassured her – Hello Kitty shouldn't worry. Tammy knew she'd been really busy. She told Hello Kitty about the costume she was going to wear for the parade; she was going as a witch! Oooh! How exciting; and it gave Hello Kitty an idea for her own costume...

But Hello Kitty still wanted to make up for missing today; no matter what Tammy said! Tammy started to protest, but Hello Kitty stopped her. She would make it up to her – she absolutely *promised!*

Hello Kitty went back to her room. What could she do? Maybe she could get Tammy a special present? She tipped the contents of her piggy bank out on the floor.

Just then, Mimmy walked past and asked her what she was *doing.*

Hello Kitty told her what had happened as Mimmy came into the room. She explained how much she wanted to make it up to Tammy, so she was going to buy her the stationery set

that she had been looking at – the one with all the glitter. Hello Kitty counted her money; she would just have enough!

Mimmy smiled; she knew Tammy would love it.

Hello Kitty did wish there was something else she could do though. Something **extra** special to show how sorry she was...

Hmmm. Mimmy thought hard. Maybe she could do something at the Halloween parade?

That was it! Hello Kitty could make Tammy a cake and present it to her after the prize-giving. Then she could ask everyone to sing Happy Birthday to her!

Mimmy smiled even wider; that would be brilliant, and the **perfect** end to the parade! At that moment, Mama came in to wish the girls goodnight. It was time for bed.

Mimmy gave Hello Kitty a hug and skipped off. Hello Kitty jumped into bed and snuggled down under her duvet thinking about Tammy's birthday surprise. It was perfect. Tammy would have a really special day.

As she drifted off to sleep, Hello Kitty vowed she would never forget a friend's birthday ever again. No matter how busy she was!

5

Disaster!

Later in the week, the day of the parade

dawned bright and sunny. Hello Kitty bounced

out of bed. Had they organised everything in

time? She, Susie and Claudia had put bunting

out the day before and the grown-ups were

doing the rest that morning. They just had to do some final decorating of the prize table and hang up the blown-up balloons.

It was nearly **all done!**

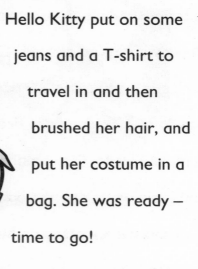

Hello Kitty put on some jeans and a T-shirt to travel in and then brushed her hair, and put her costume in a bag. She was ready — time to go!

As Hello Kitty arrived at the parade, she felt

very proud. Everything looked totally super!
The bunting blew gently in the wind and chairs
and tables were all lined up. The grown-ups
had set up a table to register people who were
entering, and a few people in costumes were
already gathered around. There were mummies,
rock stars, princesses, and werewolves. There
was **even** someone dressed as a giant
pumpkin! Hello Kitty wondered where Claudia
and Susie were, and the band and the balloons.

Then she felt a tap on her shoulder!

Hello Kitty spun round. It was Tammy and
Fifi! Hello Kitty couldn't keep the smile off her
face as she saw her friends.

Fifi was dressed in a blue skating dress with sparkly sequins that shone like diamonds. Tammy was wearing a witch's hat and cape, and carrying a broom. They both looked

amazing!

They had come along early to see if Hello Kitty needed any help, Tammy explained. They were so thoughtful! Hello Kitty reached into her bag and pulled out Tammy's birthday present and passed it to her.

She hoped Tammy liked it, and she was so sorry it was late.

Tammy looked surprised and clapped her hands excitedly. She exclaimed in delight as she saw the stationery set. It was **JUST** what she wanted! But Hello Kitty shouldn't have got it for her, she said – she'd already given her the playlist with Fifi. Tammy had been listening to it all the time!

Well… that had been Fifi rather than her, explained Hello Kitty. And she knew how much Tammy liked the stationery set, so she thought she'd get it for her. Tammy gave her a big hug

and Fifi joined in too. They both smiled at
Hello Kitty.

   Hello Kitty was so pleased! She winked at
Tammy. She had *another* birthday surprise
for her too, she told her. But Tammy would

Hello Kitty and friends

have to wait till after the parade to find out

what it was... Now though, Hello Kitty needed

to go and find Susie and Claudia. She needed to

find out where the balloons and band were.

Fifi pointed at a table behind them. Wasn't

that a load of balloons over

there? **Sure** enough,

there was a big pile

of balloons with a

pump and some

string. None of the balloons had been blown up.
Oh no! They had been supposed to be ready by
now. What had *happened?* She glanced
round. More and more people were arriving.

Tammy and Fifi waved her away. She needn't
worry! They could blow them up while she
found Susie and Claudia. It
was no problem at all.

Hello Kitty smiled gratefully and thanked them both.

She hurried away to find the other girls. When she saw them, Claudia and Susie were chatting by the judging tables. They called out hello when they spotted her.

Hello Kitty waved, and raced over. What had happened to the balloons? They weren't blown up!

Susie gasped. The balloons – oh no! She clapped her hand to her mouth. She'd completely forgotten! She started to race off to do them, but Hello Kitty stopped her. Susie didn't need to worry – Hello Kitty's friends Fifi and Tammy were doing them.

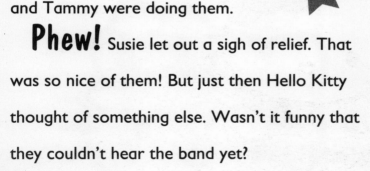

Phew! Susie let out a sigh of relief. That was so nice of them! But just then Hello Kitty thought of something else. Wasn't it funny that they couldn't hear the band yet?

Claudia looked a bit confused. The band?

Hello Kitty was puzzled. Hadn't Claudia been going to sort the band out? Didn't she remember?

Claudia threw her hands in the air. **Oh no!** She had been so busy that she had forgotten!

Hello Kitty was a bit worried. If there was no band then there would be no music for the parade. Whatever could they do?

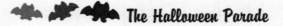

THe HALLoWeeN PARADe

They were going to have to tell the grown-ups. Susie and Claudia looked upset. Everyone had been so **excited** about the band! Claudia couldn't believe she had forgotten.

Hello Kitty put an arm around her and thought hard. All of a sudden, she remembered

something Tammy had said earlier. That was
it! She gasped and looked at them both, and a
smile crept over her face. It was all going to be
OK!

6

Halloween Parade!

Hello Kitty was about to explain her plan to

Claudia and Susie but just then Fifi and Tammy

raced over.

There they were! Fifi and Tammy had been

looking for the three of them. The balloons

Hello Kitty and friends

were all blown up and they had asked Hello Kitty's grandpa to hang them up. They'd put some streamers out on the table too… Fifi looked at Claudia and Susie. What was the *matter?*

Hello Kitty started to explain that they had forgotten about booking the band! But it would be OK – Hello Kitty had an idea! Tammy had her music with her, didn't she?

Tammy realised what Hello Kitty was thinking.

They could use her new playlist! It would be

perfect!

What a great idea! Fifi clapped her hands

with **happiness.**

Tammy got her music player out of her

pocket. What were they waiting for? They

needed to go and find one of the grown-ups!

They all went to find them, with Hello Kitty leading the way. Mama and Papa were talking to the main organiser of the parade, who was selling the tickets. Hello Kitty **explained** what had happened, and that they were really sorry there wasn't a band but they had thought they could use Tammy's music instead. Would that be OK?

The man **smiled** down at them all. That sounded fine! The sound system was all set up. Papa offered to go and make sure it all worked, and Hello Kitty hugged him and said thank you.

Mama smiled at them all too. It was a pity about the band, but they had done really well by

coming up with a solution so quickly. Susie and

Claudia both pointed at Hello Kitty – she had

saved the day, they said together!

Hello Kitty blushed, and

shook her head firmly. It

had been all of them!

And Fifi and Tammy had

helped loads as well. She

gave her other friends

a grateful look as music

blasted out from the speakers.

It looked like the parade was about to start!

Hello Kitty, Susie and Claudia quickly raced off

to get changed.

When they were dressed, Claudia turned to Hello Kitty. *Oooh,* her costume looked great! Hello Kitty smiled, and said she was going to go find Fifi and Tammy — she wanted to surprise Tammy with her costume! Was that OK?

Of course! Susie and Claudia both grinned. They would see them all later!

Hello Kitty raced off to find her friends as the other girls ran off.

There they were! Hello Kitty raced up and tapped Tammy on the shoulder; she turned around and gasped! Hello Kitty was dressed as a black cat – the perfect match to her witch costume! Tammy and Fifi both laughed and gave her a hug.

Hello Kitty smiled. She was **still** sorry she'd been so busy organising everything – but she was glad they were there with her too.

Tammy and Fifi beamed at Hello Kitty. There was no need to be sorry. It didn't matter at all!

Hello Kitty beamed right back at them; she had thought of a **new** Friendship Club rule!

What was it? Fifi and Tammy both asked eagerly – so she told them.

Good friends walk in when other people walk out.

Hello Kitty *and friends*

Hello Kitty explained that while other people could be friends too, this new rule meant that your **good** friends were always there for you even when other people forgot.

And now – it was time to get marching!

They glanced round at the people parading down the street. There was every kind of

Halloween costume you could imagine – from monsters and football players, to superheroes and dinosaurs. Mimmy was dressed as a princess, while Tammy's brother Timmy was a robot! And the giant pumpkin was marching along with his legs sticking out the bottom of his costume – he looked so funny!

Everyone was celebrating and the sound of excited laugher filled the air. Hello Kitty, Fifi and Tammy joined in, **dancing** along. Lots of people had turned out to line the streets and cheer. Hello Kitty never wanted it to end, but all too soon, they reached the finishing line and it was time for the winner of the best costume to announced. Grandpa and Miss Davey had made their decision!

And the winner is....

In first place, it was

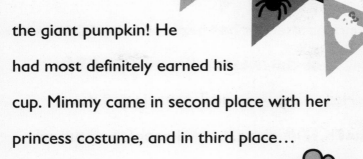

the giant pumpkin! He

had most definitely earned his

cup. Mimmy came in second place with her

princess costume, and in third place...

It was Tammy!

Hello Kitty and Fifi *cheered* as

Tammy went up to collect her prize – a big

box of chocolates. As Tammy was at the

front, Grandpa made another

announcement. It had been Tammy's birthday

this week too; would everyone **please**

join him in singing Happy Birthday to her?

He stepped aside, and there was Tammy's

enormous surprise birthday cake!

Tammy gasped and turned to Fifi and
Hello Kitty. She looked embarrassed but also
delighted as everyone sang to her, and then she
cut the cake.

Tammy ran over to where Fifi and Hello Kitty
were grinning. That had been the **best** birthday
surprise ever, and now, it was time for cake!

Hello Kitty hugged her. Wasn't that what
friends were for?

Hello Kitty and friends

Fifi and Tammy cheered. Hello Kitty hugged them both again. What a SUPER day it had turned out to be!

The end

Turn over the page for activities and
fun things that you can do with your
friends – just like Hello Kitty!

Make your own Halloween Hats!

Halloween is always lots of fun, and one of the best things about it is dressing up! Hello Kitty loves to make her own costumes, and now you can too. Follow the instructions on these pages to learn how to make your own witch's hat, and some cute cat's ears!

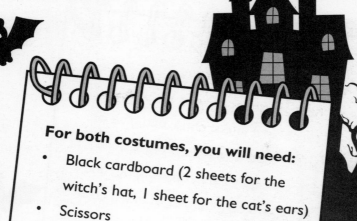

For both costumes, you will need:

- Black cardboard (2 sheets for the witch's hat, 1 sheet for the cat's ears)
- Scissors
- Sticky tape or Glue
- A ruler
- For the cat's ears, you'll also need a black headband.

Extras for decorating:

- Glitter, silver or gold pens, ribbon.

MAKE SURE YOU ASK MAMA OR PAPA TO HELP!

Boo

Witch's hat

1. Roll one sheet of your black cardboard into a cone, and glue or sticky tape it together. Make sure it's big enough to fit on your head, and leave two centimetres of extra card all around the bottom edge.

2. Trim this bottom edge so it is flat, and cut the extra two centimetres into a fringe and bend them outwards – the brim of your hat will stick to these.

MAKE SURE YOU ASK MAMA OR PAPA TO HELP!

3. Use a big bowl or other round shape to trace out your hat brim on the second sheet of card. Make sure it's bigger than the bottom of your cone so you can have a brim! Cut a hole in the middle big enough for the cone to fit in.

4. Slide the cone through the hole, and stick the bent out tabs underneath the bottom of the brim! Ta da – you now have your very own witch's hat!

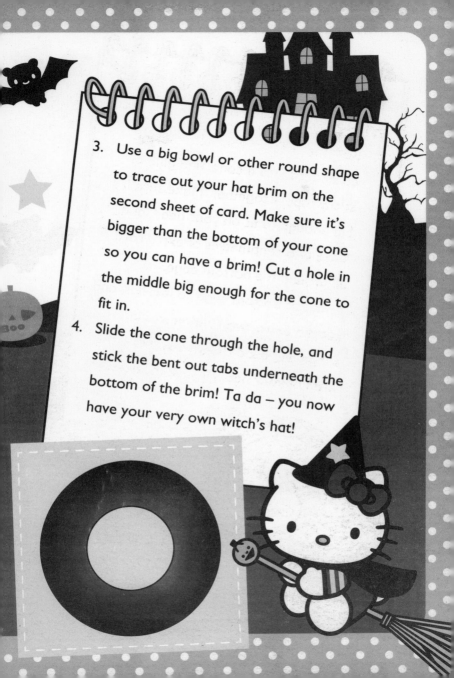

Cute Black Cat Ears

1. Measure and cut two of the below shapes out of your black cardboard

2. Place the ears on to the headband where you want them to sit, with the headband sitting where the fold line is down the middle.

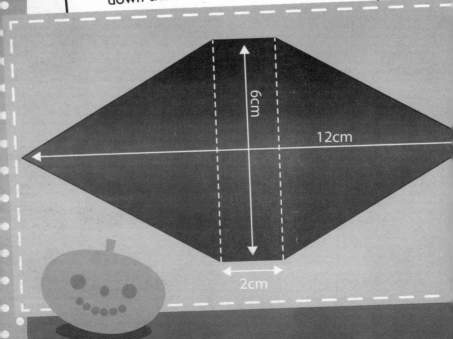

6cm

12cm

2cm

3. Glue the middle of the card to the bottom of the headband.

4. Fold the ears up around the headband, and glue them together in the middle.

5. Ta da! You now have the cutest black cat's ears, ready to wear for Halloween!

MAKE SURE YOU ASK MAMA OR PAPA TO HELP!

Finishing Touches!

Both of these ideas look great on their own, but why not finish off your costume using some of Hello Kitty's favourite tricks?

- Make your witch's hat sparkle by covering it all over in a thin coating of glue, and dusting it in glitter.

- Finish off your witch's costume by wearing a cape (you can use a blanket) and carrying a broom – remember to ask first!

- Meee-ow! Finish off your Cat Costume by using make-up to colour your nose in black, and draw whiskers on your cheeks. You'll need some grown-up help for this one...

- Why not make a tail to go with it? Fill a black stocking or pantyhose leg with scrunched up paper until it looks like a long tail, and tie the end. Attach it from the back of your clothes at the top of your bottom, and Ta da – just like a real cat!

Turn the page for a sneak peek at

Hello Kitty

and friends'

next adventure...

The Magazine Mix-Up

Hello Kitty swivelled around in the chair and
waved at Mama and her sister, Mimmy. They
were sitting on the side in The Gloss and Gleam
Hair Salon, waiting their turn while Hello Kitty
had her hair cut. The hairdresser sprayed Hello
Kitty's hair with water and then – snip, snip,
snip! Hello Kitty couldn't wait to see what she

would look like. She was sure her new haircut would be totally SUPER!

Hello Kitty was holding a shoe box on her lap. She took a little peek inside; wrapped in tissue paper were a pair of perfect black shoes with little bows on them. They were for school and Hello Kitty LOVED them.

She put the lid back down. She really wanted to try them on again, but Mama had said she had to wait — the start of school was only two days away. Hello Kitty let out a happy sigh. Getting back to school where she got to be with all her friends again — what could be better than that? Fifi, Dear Daniel and Tammy were her very BEST friends. Together with Hello Kitty they made up the Friendship Club – they met after school and in the holidays to do all sorts of fun things like baking, arts and crafts, having makeovers – and making up mottos about friendship. After the hair cut Hello Kitty was meeting up with them all at the ice-cream parlour.

Hello Kitty swung back round. The haircut was nearly finished now! The hairdresser turned to Mama White and asked if she should cut off any more. Mama White looked at Hello Kitty but Hello Kitty said that she thought that it was short enough – she still wanted to be able to put her hair bow in it! She always wore a hair bow on the left hand side of her head and her twin sister, Mimmy, always wore one on the right so people could tell them apart...

Find out what happens next in...

Out now!

Collect all of the Hello Kitty and Friends Stories!

Christmas Special: Two Stories in One!

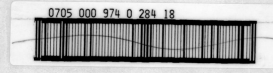